IOT MAKES IMAGINATION- THE REALITY

A NEW WAY TO DO SOMETHING

VANEE JAIN

I want to Dedicate my first book to my parents for always guiding
and motivating me in my hard times .

Contents

CHAPTER ONE

Smart mirror-A time saver

One day Misti went to market for shopping , However she has less time as it becomes very difficult for her to gave some time in these activities as she has her office work also . As she was roaming in the market she went to a shop and ask to show some cloths, she selected some items and put them aside to get a trial of the same. Due to the shortage of time she thought that it will take much time of her to try each item. She thought for a while and the time she could gave-got frustrated and went out of the shop.......

As she was going to the roadside she saw some people gathered on the roadside ....curious misti move to the roadside to find what was happening and when she reach near the crowd ....she saw an advertisement campaign is run by a sales agent of the new mall.

Being listening to the conversation misti first can't believe what she heard. The sales agent is promoting a product which will act as a time saver for the person who cannot gave much time in shopping and are genuinely faces the issue of time shortage when they want to get a trial of the cloths to make a selection i.e., A Smart Mirror.

......yes , you heard correctly a smart mirror , under which by just clicking a button it shows your entire look after wearing the cloth you want to try in the mirror . You just have to enter the particular colour and design and click on the below button named ' How you look '.And it will show your entire look after you wore the particular cloth.

Misti could not believe on his ears and this product ...she never thought or heard about any such thing before. She went to the mall to saw this amazing mirror and to get a trial of the same. She move to the counter and selected some of liked items and stand near the mirror ....as guided by the salesman she enter all the particular design, colour, and item no. on the screen and click the button named ' how you look ' . As she click the button she was surprised to see that the dress she liked will show on the body just like it will if she wear the dress in real .she was surprised and happy to see this – the way the technological advancement plays the role in making our more easy by making the things more convenient and also how it benefited the business is really very recommendable.

This mirror will not only gave the buyer a more clear picture about their entire outlook after wearing their selected item just clicking a button but also helps the seller and the buyer to save a lot of time as the buyer can also take decisions very easily and quickly and the seller can also succeed in making a lead by reducing the trial and the buyer influencing time.That's why it is known as -

' Smart Mirror – A time saver '.

CHAPTER TWO

Education sector – a new source of identification

During the month of feburary, Ashi was preparing for her final exams. As she was a B.tech student she was extremely obsessed with the emerging role of technology in various sectors which not only makes the human life easy but also gave a huge contribution to the different sectors of businesses.

As she went to gave her first exam to the exam centre ......she observed a identity verification team who came up to verify the identity of each student by scanning their question paper,admit card, and answer sheet . However it normally takes 5-7 minutes for every student. But this duration really matters during the exam time.

After she got free from her exams ......she went to her aunt house to enjoy her vacations. One day she along with her aunt move to the nearby museum. The museum has an amazing collection chof unique and rare pieces of stones which has got found in the early times and thus named 'The treasure findings'. However, there were some cases of theft of stones from the museum also in the recent days which leads in ensuring of tight security for the rare stones by the owners.

Ashi along her aunt reach at the entry gate took the token of $5 each for both of them .She then move towards the constable for security purpose through security machine .As she was fulfilling all the requirements ,An idea suddenly strikes in her mind –

' How it will be if we use a kind of Security Machine as a device to verify the identity of students during their exams ' . Yes ,you heard right , a device which will be located at different exam centres and will be use for the purpose of Identity Verification of students which will not only saves the valuable time of students but also is fast and efficient to send to the results of identity verification to the university just after all the students got verified .

This device will have a camera for face recognization at the top, a fingerprint scanner below the top camera and a bar code scanner situated at the bottom which scans all the required documents of the students including their Admit card, answer sheet and the question paper Number which is written at the top of every question paper .

This device will make the work of verification fast as well as more efficient , saves the time by verifying the identity of students and also reduce the need of a student identity verification team .

After reaching home along with her aunt,misti told her idea to his aunt who was very delighted with the same . Next day,she went to her college and talk to her principal about her views .....after having a discussion with her. The principal thought of giving it a chance and told misti to work on this as a project in your academic criteria with the guidance of your experienced teachers .

Hence misti began to work on this idea which will show the new role of tech. in the education industry .

• 5 •

CHAPTER THREE

Transportation – Brings something different and out of the box.

While travelling through the bus as to reach from one place to another is sometimes becomes very difficult due to excess of passengers with the actual capacity of the bus . Moreover the passengers also face a lot of Inconvenience not only by hanging on the hangers but also when they have to buy the tickets in huge rush from the conducter as there are also the chances that money fell down on the floor or theft by the another person by monitoring you purse or luggage .

This issue is also faced by Raju who is an MBA student and a dialy passenger of the bus route, travel from meerut to hapur . On facing the same issue, he thought that 'Is there could be any solution of this problem ' . He want to work on this problem and therefore looking for some sources and discuss this issue with his friends. However, after some days he went to a picnic by leaving this issue aside for some time .....as he was unable to find solution for the problem .

As he was wondering in the streets of Nanital(the place where he went with his friends) he took a great exposure by indulging in various activities like rock climbing, Outdoor games, mountain games, boating etc. After enjoying all of that he and his friends got very tired and went to a bakery shop to take rest and have a meal .On the shop they order some food and one of them moves to the cold drink van to have the cold drink. Raju was looking his friend how he deposit money in the van and take the cold drink and here an idea came up in his mind, ' How it will be if we use a device of the similar kind in the transportation sector .

Yes, you heard right due to excess number of passengers in the bus many problems are to be faced by the passengers. Therefore, If we install a device outside the bus door which accepts the money and other details of the passengers who wants to travel in the bus and hand to hand gave them their tickets would be very useful in solving these problems. The passengers have their tickets while they enter in the bus and are free from the inconvenience faced by them early.

This device is also very helpful for the investigation department as it provides the required information about the passenger in the case of crime, murder, kidnapping etc i.e., where the passenger took the bus , how many hours he spent, where he leave the bus , his routine timings and also his location if so are required by the Department .

He work upon this idea and discuss it later with his friends and guides and finally ......He become successful in this and sets a new example of innovation relates the Superb integration of IOT in the Transportation sector which makes the travelling experience of passengers far better .

CHAPTER FOUR

Innovation in the Hospitality sector.

Hospitality sector is growing very fast in the 21st century, and thus the increasing demand of event management is also. It's been a joyful occasion to attend someone's happy moments, involving in activities like singing, games , dancing, preparing , and eating a lot of tasty food But while eating, it becomes very inconvenient for the people to stand and eat the food ......in case they sat on the chair they have to roam again and again to the food stall if they want something more in their plate.

Tarun is a student at TMK university,Delhi went to puna to attend his brother 's wedding and while having food he faces this issue and think of an idea to solve this issue. He talk to his friends , also applies brainstorming technique to solve this issue . He also took feedback of various people about the different ideas that came up in his mind .

As he thought of a number of ideas, an idea to apply a sensor below the plate came up in his mind. It become very convenient for the people eating food if they get a stand which automatically opens by just pressing the button which is attached in the sensor and adjust according to the hand movement of the person therein.

The sensor will be attached in the middle of the plate to support the plate with the hand of the person fully and is also useful in the reduction of the risk involved in respect of the plate fell down or the food, or the food may also fell on the person's cloth eating the food.

This little innovation will help to solve a common problem faced by the persons while having meal in the family functions. And is also a small innovation of IOT in the hospitality sector which may also helps in improving the services of persons involved in the various events, increase their valuable goodwill and performance in business and also help to increase the customer satisfaction and getting good feedback from them .

CHAPTER FIVE

Design thinking in the households.

This title is itself is very weird . Yes we all are aware about household work that our mothers makes us to indulge in like washing utensils, dusting , cleaning the floor or something else.

Cleaning floor, well , according to me is the most difficult task we have to do and it becomes very inconvenient for us to sit on the floor and clean as we have to shift all the furnitures and other belongings aside again and again to clean the floor ......This shifting of our belongings not only reduces the efficieny of the work but also becomes a cause for the delay in the work done .

Rima , a B.tech student faces the same problem everyday . However she is very good in the household activities but to face the same kind of problem everyday somehow makes her think to do something regarding this issue.

Although, she was in the third year of B.tech and she is working on a project in which she develops a sensor to use the data without any human intervention . During her studies she gain a lot of knowledge about the use of technology in reducing most of the efforts in the life . As she was thinking of this household problem and along with that she was working on her project ......An idea came up in her mind " How it would works if we use a sensor in our households related work " .

Yes, you heard right. A sensor which will have a button by which we will be able to make our furnitures on either in the air for sometime or we can shift them at one corner or we can also make some furnitures like sofas , desk, table to rotate so that we can clean their other sides also which could not be possible due to their fixed place by just clicking a button and a scroller so as to control the movements of the furniture in the households.The above sensor is another example of how IOT will play an important role for the growth and development of Business . Afterwards Rima discuss the same with her teachers and start working upon it .

She also becomes successful in making the same and go for a trial also ......However there are some changes need to be made but it later proves to be a successful innovation and sets an another example of IOT for business development .

Rima named this sensor – ' Clean like Rin (soap) '

CHAPTER SIX

Innovation in the Health Care :

One day Nishi along with her sister went to the doctor for the regular checkup as her sister was suffering from depression . Her sister faces this problem from the last 5 months and her situation is not really good .

She now is not also able to talk to her family and share what she was actually thinking . Nishi is very sad after seeing her sister situation and genuinely wants to do something for her

Nishi however is a MBBS student and was in the 4th year, She had a lot of hardwork to reach this stage but she was really demotivated after seeing her sisters condition and want to do something .

Her friend named jyoti , who is a teacher and also works in an NGO named 'The Bright Future' came up to meet her .....As she talks with her,Nishi told jyoti about her sister's condition and her inability to do something. However , jyoti tries to motivate her and told about the various activities the naughty children of her NGO indulge in . Nishi also starts to enjoy the same after listening to the kid's entertaining talk .

As jyoti began to continue , she told Nishi about one of the kid name ' Rinky' who is a 5 year old girl and was known to be a Silent gem in the ' Bright future NGO 'as she remains silent in front of everyone , she was excellent in studies and most strange fact that she was the most talkative personality in front of whom .....' Guess ' ! – , It sounds funny but it is only when she talks to her teddy - bear.

Yes , the girl who remains silent in front of everyone not a single sentence came from her side is the most talkative one in front of a teddy-bear . We can say this that it's the mind of a kid .

Nishi as she had listen to this , Immediately got an idea ......she thought that sometimes when a person is in trouble is not able to share his/her problem with his/her dear ones but may comfortably shares the same with some stranger , may be due to the assumption that no one will judge him/her.

She then thought that ' how it would be if we apply a sensor in a soft toy . So that it is able to gave some response if we tries to talk with them . In the situatons like depression – where a person reach into a phrase that he/she can't able to talk to their dear ones also . Talking to a non-living toy may make a change . It could be strange when hear from something but this strange act may help in dealing with the worse condition of going into depression .

Talking to a Non-living toy rather than a strange person have several benefits – the person information shared by another person will not be leaked, misuse or transmitted elsewhere and a non-living object will be available at all time . After thinking of the same Nisha decides to do something .

She has detailed knowledge of human phsycology and therefore she decides to work upon this plan . She went to her friend name Rohit – who is a great engineer doing outstanding in his field .

After he had a ward and listen to the situation and idea as thought by Nishi. He decides to help her and therefore he also talks to his seniors at the workplace to work on this . They both with the help of rohit's guide start working on the same and finally after almost 5 months . They are ready with their sensor and now it's the time to gave it a try .

They take all the information and details to the National Medical Research Lab for conveying their idea and work to them . The senior Dr. after listening to their idea gave them the freedom to implement it.

After taking the permission , they reach to a hospital as told by the Dr. and talk to the docters there and finally , they began with the treatment of a patient name prisha...... they fits the sensor in her toy and leave her with it . As the doctors of prisha said she starts taking to the toy and the best part is, after a month – She also starts responsing to the docter's questions and also talk to her family .

Happy to listen this improvement , Nisha thought that now she can help her sister to deal with her serious problem .....so she also starts her treatment in the same hospital and hence , as expected her sister is also able to share her thoughts with the toy, with her dear one and also with nishi . After 4 months she completely manages to came out with the depression and live a happy and normal life with her family .

CHAPTER SEVEN

Innovation in the fashion field :

Rina is a graduate and want to do something in the fashion industry , she went to banglore to stay with her sister for further education . She enroll in a fashion related course to make her future in the fashion field . However as she started her studies she came up with some problems which normally every girl faces mainly while getting ready and going to attend any family function.

The time it takes to get your hair straight, curl or any specific hair style you want to have is really becomes a difficult task to do .

As she came to know about this problem , she thought that " is there can be any solution of this problem or not " .

Her sister is an engineer having a valuable experience in the same field , as Rina discuss the issue with her . She also agrees with it .

Rina one day was getting ready to go to a friend's party and therefore uses a hair straightner to set her hair . As it takes almost 1.5 hour to straighten her hair and she wishes how good it would be if by just one click these hairs can be straighten .

She told this thought to her sister ......who later discuss it with her guidemates and they decided to try this once. She and her team mates develops a plan, works upon the software required , share this idea with the head and after receiving the permission to perform the task they finally starts implementing it . They undertook all the details and the required information to finish their work .....they also took certain experiments and learn from the previous researches , they also took customer opinon into account to improve themselves .

After several months , they presents a model of the same to their boss . The boss is however surprised to see that there could be any such thing really . However , its time to gave the first trial.

They tried this to some senior womens after they grant their permission for the same......its show some changes required to be made . After making the required changes , they then experimenting it with another people multiple times .....and works upon it continuously and finally they become successful but upto some extent .

A sensor will not solve the problem but a hair setting machine will do it . Yes, a sensor may require some transmission signal from the person's body to work with which will not possible .Therefore , there can be a device which will look like a straightner having several options i.e.., one device for all the hair setting options – to straighten the hairs , to trim them , to colour them , to make a hair style , to curl them etc . This will provide all in one solution to the persons need them . It also save the expenditure that the person have to incurred in buying these things for different use. This will also reduce the need to take along multiple things with you when you are going to make someone ready.

CHAPTER EIGHT

Innovation in the retail Sector :

One day Rohan went to the market to buy a pair of new slippers for her Grandfather. After taking the slippers he came back to home and hand them over to his grandfather .

After a few days , his grandfather suffers from the pain problem in his palms and told the same to Rohan. Rohan however first told the grandfather to take some medicines and do some exercise for few days and then we will see what is the result of this pain.

His grandfather after following his advice start to take some painkillers and do some pain relief exercises also, However , he has got some relief in his palm but the pain is back after some days and bearing it when moving he stands for a longer time , or walk for a longer time is become a regular problem for his Grandfather .

Rohan got very surprised to see this as there had been no such issue of any pain in the palm faced by his grandfather and now he has to deal with it as a regular problem .

He visits to the docter name ' kamal kumar goel ' was a famous docter in that area and is known for his successful treatments .Grandfather was also there with Rohit and raise his concern about the issue and also the previous scenario . The docter after listening to the issue advice him to not wear these slippers again and take rest for a few days at home by avoiding the unneccessary movements .

After some days Grandfather starts feeling some positive results ......His pain was gone , he does not have to face it when he stands for a longer time or walks for a longer time . He was now feeling better .

Rohit was very upset to see this that he brings his grandfather's slippers and he has to suffer from the pain due to him .

However he was a B.tech student and was in the final year working on a project of Implementing the use of technology in the business . He was trying new innovations of the tech use in the business .

Taking the role of technology in the business he want to innovate something different which will help to deal with the issues of the general public . He thought of something which could be really solve the problems of the general public . But he was not able to get anything to think and therefore to work upon that .

As he was worried for this he starts feeling demotivating for that therefore he does not even seems to be happy for a longer time which also now start affecting his health .

The grandfather after seeing this becomes worried and thought that he should talk with him regarding the issue faced by Rohan .

In the evening itself he sat in the dinning hall and call him to talk . Rohit sit with him and refuse the fact that he was very worried for something thinking that the grandfather may also got worried due to him.

But as the grandfather forces , he told him that he was not getting any idea for his project and is very upset with the fact ......Grandfather told him that for not further stress and motivates him by saying that everyone has to gave some to things – sooner or later they will definitely get back to normal . He further add on by making him realizing the fact that few days before as you already know we have faced the issue of the regular pain in my palm .....Despite the fact that I had not suffer from any such problem previously and see what was the cause we find behind it ....sometimes it makes me laugh that it was the slippers due to which I had to suffer from the same .

There comes an idea in the Rohit's mind that is How it could be if the slippers can be adjusted according to the person's comfort zone and they can also make changes if they want to use it as a normal slipper or want to increase the height of the slippers while visiting a friend's house , a party or any function . This will be an awesome innovation which will help to general public as it has also faced by them somehow I their routine life .

This will not only provide them with the slippers of their own terms , but also they didn't have to carry different pairs of slippers when they went to attend any kind of wedding or some other function for a few days .

It will further help to reduce the expenditure incurred by them on buying different varieties to represent themselves in different occasions .

As he present his idea to his teachers , they feel very surprised about the existence of any such thing and also commits to guide him in this project and finally he start working on his project .

After some days he develops he develops a sensor and a mobile application with the help of one of his senior who was a great application developer. The sensor which will be attached in the slippers of the person and the details regarding the size of the same will be shown in the app and the person can make necessary changes in their slippers through the various options available in the app.

CHAPTER NINE

Innovation in the Human Resource :

Yami is a new employee in the organization name TYK limited as an Hr executive .....she began his work after proper training provided by the organization .However she has done her graduation from UKP institute of management , Delhi and now she wants to gain some industrial experience . While doing the work she had a given a task of taking the interviews for the organization – But as she begins , she faces an issue on a regular basis while calling some candidates to take the interview who are not answering the call in the first time .

The problem is that in case any candidate is not answering the call he has to gave a special note for the same and keep them highlighted and as the number are also unsaved (as there are a large number of candidates).

In case yami is on a leave or her laptop is facing any issue and any candidate calls back who has not answered before , she has to first go through her excel data (which she saved on her mobile phone) for further talk ....It becomes really irritating sometimes to first open the data and then go through it and then talk . Further , the candidate is also felt strange when she asks to tell their name (so that she may verify the data) – they say that you have called them , provide your intro, why they have to reveal their name (as the candidate doesn't know that it was an Interview call) . Sometimes , there occurs some network issues also.

Yami told the issue with her employer and later it has been discovered that the same issue is faced by all the persons who work in the HR department . After come through this issue , the head of the department thought of any measures to overcome this issue . Later , they convey this issue to top level heads who calls a meeting of all the heads of different department – Finance , Marketing , operations , IT , Human resource etc to discuss the issue faced by the HR ......After a long discussion , the IT department heads gives an opinion that this issue can be solved by developing a software for the HR .

As it will only possible to go through this problem through an application which is also connected with your laptop . The application has a feature which will have an automatic data saver installed in it through which if any person is not answering the call before and calls back later then ' A message will automatically shows on the screen of your phone having details about – when you called them recently, What was the purpose of the same , What was the response of that particular candidate . Also the same software have a transmitting information system in it with the help of which the respective person data will be automatically gets highlighted on the laptop screen of the Employee .

The idea was acknowledged greatly in the meeting and the top level gaves the project to the IT department to work on the software .

A team of employees involves some of the IT department and some of the HR department is formed so that IT employees can work according to the requirements of HR department .

After some time they become successful in developing a software to attain their objective of solving the HR department issue . They dictates the terms and features to the HR department and also presents it to the top level and requests them to implement the innovation in the HR department . The top level gaves the permission to implement it by giving an introduction of the software to the HR Employees. After the introduction , they began to work with the help of the software and gradually they saw the positive changes while they are working – The software not only helps to increase the flexibility of the employees but also increase their work efficiency and also helps in reducing the required time to do the same work by the HR department .

The IT department gets the topmost ranking to do well in that particular year and this collaboration of IT and HR department helps the business to further grow and earn more profits in the business and also maintain their market leadership and goodwill and sets a new example to using IOT for Business development in a different way .

CHAPTER TEN

A Guide For Your Appearance :

Rishita is a 5.4 tall girl living in Barelly. She has done her graduation in BBA from HIL institute , Delhi and prefers to have a simple and sober lifestyle. But there is a problem she faces every time when she want to go in order to attend a function or any party with her friends.

As she was very simple in her lifestyle it sometimes creates a problem for her as she does not have much knowledge of the different dresses along with the appropriate jewellary and hair style and style of wearing different cloths , the footwear that suits with etc .

She also sometimes feels uncomfortable even to ask this everytime to her friends. Mita a friend of her is a B.tech student who is well known about the level of simplicity with which Rishita lives .

She thought of doing something for this but don't know how to do this . She has learn something about the use of technology in business recently in her studies and also works on a project related to that......she then thought that how it would be if use IOT in Fashion field .

She thought of building an app which will act as a guide for you so that you easily find which dress will suit with which jewellary and hair style and the suitable footwear for the outlook.

She went to her teachers and guidemates for the same and gets some useful feedback , she then meet one of her elder brother who works a well - known App developer Who shares the same to his boss and then after having a talk with him thought work upon it.

After some days he finally become successful and presents the same to his boss , after getting the approval from the boss its time to lauch this app. In the beginning it doesn't got much positive responses but as the company have made improvements according to the feedback and surveys conducted by them , It starts working and is became the most popular app, Which has got the highest Ratings and is installed by most of the Buyer's segment with the best positive feedbacks in just 5 months .

This app sets another example for the Magical integration of IOT for business development which not only helps the business to earn more profits but also help them maintain a major market share which also builds its goodwill and performance.

About The Author :

Vanee jain is a student currently pursuing MBA from ABES Business School, Ghaziabad. She has done her graduation in B.com from R.K college, Shamli. She has also engage in a Mini Project includes her own startup idea name " Network to Net worth " in which her aim was to build a network of Small Business owners as to guide them for the growth and expansion of their businesses. So, that they can also earn a big name in the Industry.